I

A Short Story

RAY ELLIS

"I" – A Short Story

By Ray Ellis

First Edition eBook: 2012
First Edition Paperback: 2013
ISBN (eBook): 978-1-938596-04-9
ISBN (Paperback): 978-1-938596-18-6

Cover design by Ray Ellis II
Published in the United States of America
NCC Publishing
Meridian, Idaho, 83642, USA
www.nccpublishing.com

20131002

"And be not afraid of them that kill the body, but are not able to kill the soul: but rather fear him who is able to destroy both soul and body in hell."

Jesus
Matthew 10:28 ASV

Chapter One

I was five years old. I don't even remember where the thought had come from. But there I was, sneaking around back to see if I could catch Wanda in the outhouse before she pulled up her underwear.

***

The darkness pressed in on me, heavy and liquid. Although I knew I was alone, I could feel Him staring at me, watching me, His gaze penetrating the darkness as easily as if it had been noon. His eyes seeing me. Knowing me. Understanding my every thought, even as it formed in my mind.

The sound of dripping water echoed off what sounded like a cavernous vault. Drip. Drip. Drip. Teasing my thirst. My throat felt raw and parched. The stone slab I awakened on felt cold beneath me, but the surrounding air was hot, laced with a heavy sticky humidity—but no water pooled. No condensation dripped from the stone walls.

Standing, I hit my head on the too low ceiling. I could not rise to my full height, but had to remain crouched over from the waist. The floor, I discovered, was covered with sharp stones that cut into my bare feet as I walked hunched like Hugo's Quasimodo. Occasionally raking my head or shoulders on shards of protruding stones, I moaned with inflicted pain.

Again, the tormenting sound of water dripping unseen somewhere in the darkness tormented me. Then the question I dreaded formed in my mind: Was I to continue like this forever?

***

I was six years old when my grandmother told me the story of the Ten Commandments. I remembered sitting on her knee in the darkened room watching the glow from the wood burning stove dance across the soot-stained walls and high ceiling.

Gran-Ma threw the remains of her water against the unpainted wall and pointed to the moist darkness making its way towards the floor. "You see dhat, son? Dhat's how death came down out of heaven on the night of the first Passover. Like a cloud from God, death reached its fingers down into Egypt and killed all the first born chil'lun." She spat a caramel-colored stream of tobacco juice into the open fire before continuing. "All the firstborn's whose mamas and daddies didn't paint the doorjamb with the blood."

I swallowed as only a six year old could while hearing stories of judgment and trying my best to act innocent all at the same time. "You think God's gonna be pouring out death on us again, Gran-Ma?" I asked, feelings of desperation and fear growing in my anxious, juvenile mind.

She hugged me to herself, which smelled of Epsom salt and snuff, before putting me down. "Nahh, boy, that's why God done sent down Jesus for to die for us so's we won't have to die and go to hell."

At the mention of hell, I stopped breathing. Everybody knew about hell.

***

I found that my cell, for that's what it was, was only about ten feet by six feet across. Yet after rising from the stone slab, I could no longer find it and was forced to sit on the ragged floor. The shards and stones now cut into the flesh of my buttocks and back as I tried to rest, too tired to continue standing in the half-crouched position.

The temperature had begun to change as well, alternating in an instant from being suffocatingly hot to bone jarring cold. And still, somewhere in darkness, the sound of dripping water continued.

From somewhere in the shadows I began to hear voices—voices familiar but not. Then as if in a vision, I saw myself. I was seven years old...

"Come on," I said to Alex, a neighborhood friend, "put it under your shirt while I keep a lookout."

A few minutes later, Alex and I sat under the shade of a huge oak, enjoying the stolen fruits of our labor. He passed me a share of the honey bun he'd stolen while I passed him a bag of the plain potato chips I'd walked away with.

Leaning back on our elbows, we watched as fluffy white clouds floated by and imagined strange and wonderful shapes bounding across the azure sky. "What do you think?" I asked into the comfortable silence.

"I d-don't know," Alex began stuttering. "Maybe we shouldn't ought to of stole this s-stuff."

"Not that, stupid," I said. "Besides it's too late now; we already ate most of it. I was talking about the clouds. What shapes do you see?"

Alex sat up and looked at the almost empty potato chip bag in his hand before handing it back to me. "I see a bird...and look over there," he said pointing excitedly, "that big cloud, it looks like a dragon."

I laughed, giving myself fully to the game of make believe. "Looks like that dragon's gonna eat up that bird."

Later that evening, Mrs. Jackson walked Alex all the way back to the store. She made him tell Mr. Thompson what he'd done, that he'd stole some sweets and a package of pre-sweetened Kool-Aid from the store earlier that day. After he confessed, she whipped him right there in the store where everybody could watch.

Earlier, Alex had gone home and bragged to his brother that he'd stolen the Kool-Aid from the store. Mrs. Jackson overheard him, and well, you know the rest. One thing I can say about old Alex, though, he never told. He kept my secret to this day, and *no one* ever found out that I had stolen right along with him.

***

I was cold again. The only sound I could hear now was that of my own teeth chattering and the continual dripping of water. My feet and buttocks and back hurt all the time now. I tried to lie down, tried to sleep, but I couldn't. The cold crept into me feeling like my very bones were freezing, and then when I felt I would freeze, instantly, I was hot. Too hot.

I don't know how long I've been here. It feels like forever. Time seems to not matter or even exist. I tried counting the drips of water or my steps as I paced around my cell. I always lost track, either hitting my head or forgetting the count when the temperature changed, and I'm distracted by the new sensation of agonizing discomfort.

Desperation set in. My thirst is unbearable. I had to have something, anything to drink. Lifting my hacked and sliced feet to my mouth, I attempted to drink my own blood, only to find the cuts had not produced any bleeding but dry lacerations only.

In anguish, I cried out. My first words spoken aloud, since waking in the vile place, only to find them absorbed and sucked away into the darkness. I was alone without even the comfort of my own voice.

Again, a memory came. I was nine years old.

Chapter Two

Heat. Cold. Thirst. Pain. These are my constant companions, and the darkness—and all the time Him. Even in the heavy gloom, I feel Him staring at me, watching me, but never speaking. Anxiety gnawed at me like rats chewing on a wall, ripping an opening. Finally, I could take it no longer. I jumped to my feet preparing for the fight.

With an abruptness born of pain, I crumpled after striking my head against the low ceiling. I could feel where the protuberance had gouged into my scalp. The burning pain seared through the layers of my skin and struck bone. Dropping to the floor, curling into a fetal position, I scraped my arms, my legs, and back across the jagged surface. I screamed in pain.

"Face me!" I yelled into the darkness. "Come out and face me. You have no right to treat me like this. I've done nothing wrong." My voice was sucked away. Had I spoken aloud or was it only in my mind? "Who are you?" I screamed it again and again. Over and over. Still nothing…nothing but the incessant dripping of the unseen and unreachable water. My throat burned with acrid dryness.

***

I couldn't believe my luck; they were finally going to let me join in. "You go get some Kool-Aid for the punch," Leroy, one of the older teens told me. Lucky for me, I knew how to get Kool-Aid.

All around me other kids my age, and some older, were being given instructions. Some were told to get things from the store, like me, while others were told to bring food from the surrounding farmers' fields.

At last, night fell. With it, the bonfire was lit, and the party began. Grabbing a number-three galvanized tub from one of the back porches, I dragged it beneath the standing faucet and began filling it with water. We dropped packet after stolen packet of Kool-Aid beneath the running water and watched as the secret ingredient was added. Someone had either bought or stolen several bottles of Johnnie Walker Whiskey and, adding it to the Kool-Aid, made it the star attraction of the bedraggled meal and highlight of the summer block party.

The empty field behind my house was alive with several small fires, some cooking corn while others were used for roasting or boiling hotdogs, minus the buns. Watermelons were burst and broken open and served in chunks. The haunting lyrics of the Temptations' "Runaway Child" thumped in the way only Motown could on a summer night out under the stars. People danced, laughed, and loved. I stood in the shadows just outside the ring of fire and watched as the people I knew as family and friends played together.

In a pile off to my left stood the stacks of debris: cornhusks yet to be burned, food packaging, and melon rinds. I smiled. One of the reasons I had been invited was because of my ability to *get* certain things. "What do you think?" I asked one of the other young ones.

His eyes as big as my own, Franky nodded his head, the flicker of red-orange firelight reflecting in his brown orbs. "Yeah." It sounded more like a protracted sigh than a spoken word.

I knew exactly what he was thinking when his eyes fell on the proof of the pilfered food, but he was wrong. The farmers and the stores would never miss the little bits we had taken. Besides, it was only right that we got our little bit.

***

The silence wore on me. Was there anyone else in this place or was I doomed to be alone forever? That couldn't be forever denoted time. I don't know how I knew, but I knew time didn't matter here. It simply didn't exist.

***

The song service ended like most, with the pastor offering the invitation to join the church. "Why not tonight," he cried, echoing the refrain from the old hymn. "If you hear the Spirit's calling, don't put it off." He raised both arms above his head, the oversized sleeves hanging from his wrist and flapping like gull wings. "Come on, you." He pointed over to the congregation.

I leaned over to my little brother and snickered, "I think he's talking to you."

"Nahh, you. You're the big devil," he answered. We both laughed. That is, until Mom reached over and pinched us. She cut her eyes at us giving us *the look*.

"You boys better pay attention," she whispered through clinched teeth. "You never know, this may be your last chance to respond to Jesus," Mom said, her face now serene.

I looked at my brother and rolled my eyes, careful not to let Mama see me. We smiled at each other after she turned her face forward.

When the service had ended, we ran from the air-conditioned building into the bright summer sun, momentarily blinded by its brightness. After the short run home, we jumped, whooping and yelling from the back porch, after getting into play-clothes, and headed to the playground.

At thirteen, I was not the tallest, but I was stocky and well-built for my age. Leaning back against the rough bark of the large pecan tree, I hesitated as Jimmy, a neighborhood friend, passed me the joint. I'd never smoked marijuana before and wasn't really sure if I wanted to; after all, I was a good churchgoing boy.

"Hey, you don't have to if you don't want to, but it's here if you want it," Jimmy said.

I looked at my little brother who stood staring at me with watchdog tenacity. "None for you, little brother," I said, rubbing my fingers through his woolly hair before accepting the proffered joint. Tentatively, I placed the hand-rolled cigarette to my lips, careful to hold it pinched between my index finger and thumb, imitating my cousin and the older teens. I inhaled, sucking the sweet smelling smoke deep into my lungs; holding it in as long as I could, the heated smoke burned the back of my throat. I coughed and then giggled before passing the joint back to Jimmy.

Jimmy and I laughed, and he slapped me on my back after I'd completed my initiation. Just as the buzz reached my head, I looked at my little brother. His eyes were wide, but without the glowing admiration I'd become accustomed. This time I saw disappointment and sadness as his faith and belief in me had proven vain.

***

"Why are you showing me this?! I know what I did! I told him not to use drugs." I rubbed my hands over my face, pulling at my cheeks and clawing at my scalp, trying to remove the feeling of grime and filth that covered me. "You can't blame me for his choices!" Still, He ignored me.

Now my cell was cold; I could feel ice crystals growing, crawling along the walls of my lungs. Thirst pulled at me, burned in my throat, and now hunger gnawed at my stomach.

I tried to sleep, tried to ignore the pain just to pass the *time*. But beneath me the floor grew hot; the sharp edges feeling like teeth cutting into my flesh. My joints began to stiffen, my fingers refusing to bend or flex despite my trying, defying my constant efforts.

Unable to find peace even in sleep, I stood again and hobbled around my cell. For what must have been hours, I walked around and around, circling the small enclosure.

Drip. Drip. Drip.

The sound of the water seemed closer, but might as well have been a thousand miles away.

My stomach growled. I could smell chicken frying; the various seasonings of garlic, salt, and black pepper, mixing together reminded me of Sunday afternoon dinners. My throat burned, unable to even be moistened with spit from my mouth. Hunger was a physical pain, pulling at my gut, demanding to be satisfied, only to be denied.

"WHAT DID YOU DO WITH MY GRACE?"

The Voice was itself a presence. It echoed in my brain, becoming a pressure forcing itself against me. "Get out of my head," I yelled. Scurrying to the corner, I hid my face, ignoring the painful lacerations. I buried my head into the right angle.

I had to get away from Him.

Again, the Voice came as if from the wall, only a breath away from my face. The Voice brushed against me like a whispered kiss, yet I fell backwards onto the floor. Screaming, I scampered backwards as far as the small cell would allow. "Get out of my head! Get out of my head! I don't want you. Go away!"

The Voice came again. "I loved you and gave My life for you," It said.

The silence returned and immediately I missed the Voice. I loathed it, yet I missed it. I screamed against the void created by the absence of the Voice. With my knees pulled against my chest and my back against the wall, I cried waterless tears.

Chapter Three

Darkness pressed in on me like a physical force, crushing my chest, making each breath a tragic battle. The Voice had gone.

Rubbing my face with scarred, rutted hands, I sighed in relief to be free of the Voice. The heated stones gnawed into my back and cut into my feet. Like many times, as in my past, I figured I could get use to any situation and, in time, overcome it. I was wrong.

The heat increased, sucking the breath from my lungs. I tried to stand. Fumbling, I reached out for the wall; my legs became weak from the lack of oxygen. I screamed and fell.

The floor was ice.

***

"Come on! Hurry!"

I fled from the house. Adjusting my shirt as I ran, I jumped off the back porch and ran toward the waiting car. Eric smiled as I closed the door and we sped away.

The loud thump thump of the bass faded along with the sounds of the house party as the car turned the corner and slipped into the night. He laughed.

"Man, your mom was mad."

I looked at him, then out the window and continued fixing the buttons on my shirt.

"I sent her to another party three blocks away, but it won't take her long to figure out it's the wrong one." He looked at me and shook his head. "You don't even care, do you?" When I still didn't respond, he turned back to the road and kept driving.

After being dropped off at home, I hurried to my bedroom and curled in my bed, pulling the blankets over my head and deepening my breathing as if asleep. Shortly thereafter, my mom came into the room and flicked on the light. Groaning, I rolled away from the light and feigned sleep.

"You're not fooling me, boy! I know you ain't sleep," my mother said in that stage of anger that grips a parent's heart where once fear has been relieved. "I told you to be home by midnight. It's almost three in the morning!"

Finally, I rolled over to face her, still pretending to be waking. "What? I've been home. You weren't here when I got back."

"Don't lie to me!"

I sat up revealing my bare chest but still dressed from the waist down. "Mom, what are you talking about? I've been in bed." I knew she couldn't prove I hadn't. Below me on the bottom bunk, my brother stirred and began mumbling in his sleep. He would be no help to her.

"We're not through with this. We'll talk in the morning." She turned off the light as she left the room. I knew I should feel bad, but for now, I was just glad she had not used the belt she carried in her trembling hand. Smiling, I rolled over and settled into the pillow, preparing to sleep for real this time.

***

Darkness. Cold. Intense heat. The return of cold. Silence. But the Voice and the Speaker remained absent.

***

I was finally a senior, and graduation was only a week away. We had it all planned out. Immediately following the graduation ceremony, we both skipped out on family parties and had one of our own design.

The Sunday before graduation, Pastor Johnson stood in the pulpit preparing to deliver his baccalaureate sermon. He stared at the six of us, four girls, Eric and I; we smiled and exchanged sly glances. Lifting the white towel against his dark face, he wiped the sheen of sweat that glistened on his brow, just above his full lips.

He inhaled and swept a hand across his body, indicating the six of us in blue, red, and gold graduation robes. "There was one who thought he could out run the plans of God. Jonah was his name."

I could tell by the way he was getting wound up, he would be awhile. Besides, if I'd heard one message about some poor soul getting slapped down because he didn't do something God had told him, I'd heard a million.

Anyway, I was okay. I'd spent my entire life in church, not like those poor saps that spent their Sunday mornings standing on the street corner or moaning while trying to get over hangovers from the night before.

I sighed and settled in for a long, long afternoon.

***

As the day in question arrived, Eric was his usual self, slow to decide and needing to be shown the way. "Come on." I encouraged him. He looked at me and then back at his mother sitting around the table with the rest of his family. Finally, he nodded his head and let the screen door close softly behind him.

This time I was driving, and good thing too, because we all knew how Eric got once he'd been drinking. And, if our plans went the way we set them, there would be a whole lot of drinking going on tonight.

I slowed the vehicle, a brown over brown 1972 4-door Ford LTD, and Eric got out and opened the rear door. "Hey ladies, been waiting long?" I asked, purposely adding a sense of smoothness and what I hoped was enticement to my voice.

"I don't know," Deborah said, leaning forward, allowing us both a view of her ample cleavage. "Somebody promised me a party tonight, and I'm ready to romp."

Her friend, Sarah, held herself in reserve, not as froward as her very earthy friend. I thought I'd have to sample them both. Eric ushered Deborah into the front seat, and then followed Sarah into the rear. I met her gaze as she allowed herself to be seated before turning my full attention to the curvaceous and willing form that was Deborah.

After parking out near the lake and enjoying all the carnal delights that came as a packaged deal with Deborah, I decided to take a short walk near the tree line. There I found Sarah sitting on a fallen log, just beyond where the water pipe fed the lake from the well deep underground.

Silver moonlight reflected off the mirror surface of the water as shimmering stars danced as if in chorus overhead. From the far side of the lake, conifer trees stretched their limbs heavenward in the inverted sky as their images reflected across the still surface of the water.

I walked to where she sat reclining on the log and nestled close to her. She smiled and I brushed the side of her face with the backs of my knuckle. Her breath caught.

Once our appetites for passion had been filled, we returned to the car only to find that both Eric and Deborah sat waiting and looking for us.

"Man," Eric began, "this is low even for you."

"What? I played my usual innocent self." He didn't challenge me. He never did. Instead, he simply shook his head and turned away. I walked over to Deborah and pulled her into my embrace. She stiffened before surrendering to me, as I knew she would.

Pushing her away to arm's length, I looked into her eyes. "I thought you wanted to party. I'm here, let the party begin." Sarah started some music on the car's stereo, and I took Deborah's hand and we began to dance.

The beat of the music intensified, and I began to spin and twirl around like a child playing helicopter. I began to feel lightheaded from too much smoke and wine. Dancing, I laughed out loud, spinning until I collapsed from exhaustion.

***

Crumbling to the floor, I screamed. Hot stones tore into my flesh. The Voice had returned. "I called to you, but you would not come."

"Get out of my head!"

"I played for you, but you would not dance to My tune."

"Leave me alone!"

"I shed My blood for you, but you drank instead the wine of this world until you became drunk with her violence."

"Leave me alone!"

"I loved you."

"I don't want your love!"

"I love you still."

I cursed. "Leave me alone! Get out of my head!"

The Voice left me, and the oppressive silence returned. As much as I hated the sound of His voice, I longed for it. I missed it deeply, as if my heart had been made to sing its chorus.

I rolled to my knees and bit back another curse as the hot stones gouged into my kneecaps. I would not give Him the pleasure of my tears. "What do you want from me?" I yelled into the darkness. My throat burned from thirst, and still the sound of water continued dripping unseen in the darkness.

"What do you want? Do you want me to admit that You were right; that You won?!" I forced myself to stand in my Quasimodo crouch and shuffled around my cell. "I didn't force Eric to come with me, and both those girls got exactly what they wanted. Me."

A dry crackling sound filled my head, and I realized I was laughing. "That's it, isn't it? You're jealous that those people chose me instead of You. That they loved me more than they loved You. Ha!" I pointed a ripped and torn finger toward the ceiling.

"I beat You and there's not a thing You can do about it."

"You were a blind leader of the blind, and if you are blind then you and those that followed you will fall into the ditch."

I turned looking for someone to hit and punched the wall instead. I felt the bone in my knuckle snap, and the pain added to the inventory that was already building. "I didn't do so bad. I was successful," I said defiantly.

The darkness began to fade, growing deeper somehow. I rubbed my eyes and when I looked up again, I could see. I lifted my face and found that I was looking at the shoulder of a woman's black dress. It was Mrs. Swift, Eric's mother. Looking beyond her, I saw Eric, or rather his body.

He lay in an open casket; his gloved hands folded neatly across his chest. The charcoal gray suit had been his favorite. The mortician had done a great job; the bullet wound that had ended his life was barely visible beneath the makeup.

As I made my way back to my seat, I remember how Eric had told me he was going to see Sarah. He was so sure of himself.

"Don't do it," I'd said. I hadn't expected him to challenge me, but he had.

He stood in front of me, his feet shoulder width apart, and squared his shoulders. Lifting his chin slightly, he asked, "What? You—you're the only one that can get with that?" He poked my chest with his hand. "What, she too good for me or something?" He was angry.

"No—no...man. It's not like that. She's not good enough for *you*. You remember graduation night at the lake? I thought she was all that back then, but that girl laid down with anyone with a baggie or a bottle."

He harrumphed. "Well, I guess it's my turn, huh?" He buttoned his shirt and rubbed cologne onto his face. He had turned and smiled at me.

Reaching into my pocket, I'd thrown him a packet of condoms. "At least use protection, fool," I said chiding him.

He smiled at my use of the name we had for each other whenever one of us was doing something risky. It turned out that it wasn't the kind of protection he needed. Sarah's estranged boyfriend, fresh out of prison and carrying a grudge against the world, had discovered them together and shot them both. Eric had not survived.

***

My vision darkened again and the cold, blistering cold, returned. "You can't blame me for that," I cried in my defense against the darkness. Shaking my fist and pointing at the ceiling, I screamed, "You judge me unfair.

How can you blame me for what Eric did? He was a grown man." I cursed the Voice.

Like a wet garment, the silence hung heavy on me. I could feel its presence. It pressed against me. Even His silence was a judgment against me. I could feel His eyes boring into me, seeing my very soul, my thoughts, my imaginations, none of it hidden from Him.

"I have known you."

I turned my back to the sound of that Voice.

"Whether you were sitting down or rising from your bed, I have seen you."

I covered my ears with my hands and screamed, trying to drown out the sound of His voice; His words cutting me as sure as the stones of the floors and walls. "You don't understand what I—"

"I have understood your very thoughts even as they formed in your heart."

Clinching both fists, I shook them in His face. "You don't know me!"

"I have watched over your path, and I know all your ways."

"Get out of my head. Out of my head. Get out! Get out! Out! Out!"

"There is not a word you have spoken that I did not know it altogether. I have been behind and in front of you. I have called you, and you would not listen."

I screamed and cursed Him. "You—you judge me guilty? But your knowledge was too wonderful for me; it was too high. I could not understand it. You are not fair!"

"Where could you go and be free of My presence? Even here I Am with you."

The sound of His voice was driving me…driving me. I felt pushed, caught, corralled. I stood and tried to walk away from the Voice, but the cell offered me no escape. The Voice continued.

"If you had ascended up into heaven, I Am there. While you make your bed here, behold I Am still here."

"Leave…me…alone!"

"Even if you had taken the wings of the morning, and dwelt in the uttermost parts of the sea, even there you would have had to contend with Me."

"Arrgh!" I rammed my head against the wall trying to rid myself of that Voice, but nothing helped; nothing stopped it. It echoed in my mind and from the very air surrounding me. The sound of the accursed dripping continued, adding to my torment. And still, He just would not shut up.

"Even when you attempted to hide in the darkness, My eyes beheld you. The cover of night shown as the day around you; I saw all that you did."

Falling to the floor, I curled into a ball trying to hide from Him now.

"When I formed you in your mother's womb, even there I'd called you."

"Go away! Leave me! Leave me alone! Leave me…."

For a brief moment, the silence returned. The Voice had left me, and almost immediately, I missed it. I longed for it, and hated it all at the same time.

***

"I sent you My messengers and you would not hear them." He had returned. "You spoke wickedness and took My name in vain."

I rolled to my back, ignoring the pain in my back for the greater pain in my head and in my heart. "Please, forgive me. I'm sorry—"

"And then will I profess unto them, I never knew you: Depart from Me, ye that work iniquity."

His words had hit me like a physical blow, and then the heat returned.

***

I watched her walking toward me, the very essence of feminine beauty. The gossamer veil covering her face could not hide the radiance of her smile. As she passed the crowd, which stood to either side of the isle, they turned and followed her with their eyes and smiles. When she stopped before me, I felt my heart would burst for having won her.

"You may kiss your bride." These words began what should have been the most wonderful part of my life. When I broke the kiss, I knew deep in my heart what love really was. When I held her in my arms, I felt alive. With her, I felt complete.

***

"No," I screamed. He was taking the vision from me. All around, the darkness swirled like a cloud of dust, and the scene began to fade then change. When I looked again, I was holding a different woman in my arms and tasting her lips. "How long before your flight takes off," the strange woman whispered.

"Oh, I have an hour."

"Good."

"Good?" I asked, puzzled, yet hopeful.

She flashed a coy, seductive smile. "Good…then we have time," she never finished her sentence.

***

The Voice returned. "Yet still I loved you. Still I would have forgiven you, but you would have none of Me."

Intense heat flashed to cold and then back to heat again. The temperature changing so fast, I couldn't even begin to adjust; my continual state was pain and discomfort.

***

"Dad?!" The look on my son's face was one of unbelief and pain, then shame.

I released the woman that was not his mother, and stood stepping away from the young lady who appeared to be barely older than my son's date. "Son? What are you doing here?" I looked around the restaurant as if just seeing it for the first time. I looked past him at the door, hoping his mother wasn't with him.

"She's not here. She's where you should be."

"Wait, Boy, you don't talk to me like—"

"No, you don't! You don't have the right to talk to me like you're a father. Not now. You should be home with your *wife,* and I find you out here with this...this—" He pointed at the woman, who was still sitting at the table.

"Son, I can explain—"

"You can explain that you're cheating on Mom?"

I grabbed my son by his bicep and pulled him away from the table, leaving his date looking down at my own. The two women scrutinized each other; either of them could easily have stood as the target of my son's affection. Both remained in awkward silence. "Son, you can't tell your mother about this," I began.

He snatched his arm away from me. "You want me to lie for you? T-t-to cover for you?" His fist clenched and unclenched as he stiffened his arms at his sides.

"Don't be a fool, Boy! This would kill your mother if she found out." I looked over his shoulder at the two twenty-something ladies at the table and smiled. My date smiled and waved back at me. "This is bigger than either you or me...it's not even about me! This is about your mom. You can't tell her." I relaxed when I saw his shoulders sink and hands lying flat near the seams of his trousers. I knew then that he understood.

"God help me, I hate you right now."

"I understand. Don't get me wrong, Son, I'll make this right with God." I started back toward the table then stopped. "I'll do right by your mom too. Don't worry." He dropped his chin and shook his head in a slow defeated motion. He slumped against the wall and covered his face with his hands.

I made my way back to the table, careful to fix my smile with a look of congealed control in place. When my son first brushed passed me, grabbing his date's hand, I thought he intended to fight me. But true to his word, he simply turned and stalked away.

Smiling at the very young lady sitting across from me, I reached forward and stroked the back of her knuckles with my index finger. She looked past me toward the exit. I lifted her hand, ignoring the ring on my left index finger, and kissed it. "Don't worry, he's a smart boy. He'll do the right thing."

Chapter Four

"Therefore you are inexcusable, O man, you who judged others. For when you judged others, you condemned yourself; for you did the same things."

I was back in my cell, back in the dark, back again with His voice. "I took care of my wife," I screamed. "She had a great house and money in the bank. We took vacations every summer. She always had a nice car. I got her a new car every other year. I paid my tithes regularly and gave huge offerings. Ask the Reverend, he'll tell you all the stuff I did for that chur—"

"But you were sure, confident in yourself and in your own judgments of religious duties."

I stood up and rammed my head on the too low ceiling. "You see, even You admit it yourself, I did serve Y—"

"You thought and still believe that you will escape the judgment of God because you have somehow earned your way into My Father's grace?"

My shoulders drooped as I saw how my latest plan, my latest hope, had come to nothing. "B-but you just said I did all those wonderful things." I was beginning to sound pitiful even to myself.

"You despised the riches of My Father's goodness and forbearance and longsuffering, and thought that His goodness was a license for you to continue in your sin."

"But I—"

"But you did not understand that the goodness of God was meant to lead you to repentance."

"But I—"

"But after the hardness of your impenitent heart, you have treasured up wrath for yourself for the day of wrath where the righteous judgment of God will be poured out on you according to your deeds."

"But—b-but I was…"

"Son of man, you stand guilty."

I collapsed in a ball on the rough sharpened floor, and once again, cried waterless tears. Deep quaking sobs racked my body, and despite the heat, I could feel the cold tendrils of fear clutch at and squeeze my heart. For the first time since I'd awakened in this nightmare existence, a faint light began to show in my cell.

In spite of myself, I walked toward the light…drawn by it. As I walked, I suddenly became aware of a sea of people around me. All at once, I was just one in a vast multitude of humanity. Of course, I didn't know what I looked like, but I imagine I must have looked just like the souls around me.

The crowd all moved forward as one. Fear hung like a cloud over us. Like tendrils of an oily smoke, dread wrapped around us and pulled us forward, forcing us all down on our knees before the light that rose before us.

I don't know how I saw it, but from what seemed like many miles away, I could see in the midst of the light stood a solitary figure. But this Man sitting on a great throne looked like no man I'd ever seen before. The throne shone white with an internal luminescence. His eyes, even from this distance, pierced me as surely as if they had been spears.

In desperation, I looked around for a place to hide, for somewhere to flee, but no escape was available. I was but one person in a sea of terrified flesh.

Even before He spoke, I knew how His voice would sound. It would be *the* Voice. That same Voice I had spent a lifetime ignoring and practicing and pretending not to hear. This same, very same Voice had been my only company in the dark cell. Now the Owner of that Voice stood staring down at me.

Standing beside Him was another man, less glorious than the first, but still astonishing on his own, who held a giant blood-red book in his hands. Its gilded pages seemed to absorb the light from the man who held it, concentrated it like a lantern, and amplified it out onto the ocean of upturned, expectant faces. Everything inside me feared what was inside that book.

As the angel standing beside the throne, for that undoubtedly was what it was, began to open the book, a cry of bewailing moans rose up from the crowd. Cries turned to cursing and then muted down into pleading.

One voice rose above the cacophony of sounds. Vile cursing and swearing directed at the One seated on the throne. As I wondered who it was, who would have the audacity to speak to One so obviously holy and full of power, I realized the voice was my own.

Then the angel turned his loveless attention on me. Hatred so intense, I could feel it press against me. He pointed one finger at me and with the other traced down the page, and I knew he was looking for my name in the book.

Without speaking, he turned and looked at the One seated on the throne and shook his head, then closed the book. Even as the Seated-One opened His mouth to speak, I cried out, "But I gave in Your name. I fed the poor in Your name. I paid for missionary trips. I even helped pay for the pastor's retirement trip…I—"

"DEPART FROM ME, YE WORKER OF INIQUITY. I NEVER KNEW YOU."

"But I…"

The End

A Note from the Author

Thank you for reading the short story "I". Now that you've finished this story, I would love to hear from you. You can email me with your thoughts on the story, or friend me on Facebook. You can even sign up for my newsletter, which will give you updates on upcoming releases and all the other craziness going on in my corner of the world.

If you would like to help this story succeed, please tell others about it. You can loan your copy to a friend, and ask your local libraries and bookstores to order it.

In addition, if you post a review on Amazon.com, it would be very helpful.

My email address is:
ray@rayellis-author.com
You can follow my every day thoughts on my blog at:
http://authorray.blogspot.com
Follow me on Twitter at:
Twitter@RayEllisNHI

Other Books by
Ray Ellis

Notorious - A Nate Richards Novel - Book One.
Previously released as N.H.I. (No Humans Involved)

Dead List - A Nate Richards Novel - Book Two.
Previously released as D.R.T. (Dead Right There)

Insidious - A Nate Richards Novel - Book Three.

These books are available in eBook format and in print on Amazon.com, or at your favorite eBook retailer.

Look for ***Cave of the Kraken***, a science-fiction thriller due for release in winter of 2013/2014.

About the Author

Ray Ellis is a veteran law enforcement officer, former Marine, and ordained Christian pastor. Ray began his career in law enforcement with the Orange County Sheriff's Department in the city of Orange, California in 1989. After working for a number of years in the maximum security facility, he transferred to patrol, working along Orange County's coast as well as the inner canyons and barrios.

After eight years in Orange County, Ray moved to Idaho and continued his law enforcement career where he has served as a patrol officer, detective, and officer instructor for the Idaho POST Council. In 1999 Ray was appointed as a primary instructor for the Idaho POST Academy Police Training Institution for Idaho, instructing on subjects of arrest control, cultural diversity, and instructor development. From 2007-2011, Ray served as the lead sex crimes investigator for the agency where he works.

Ray is active in the writer's community in Idaho and has recently served as the president of the Idahope Writer's Group. In 2011, Ray was selected as one of the

Top Fifty Authors in the state of Idaho, and then in 2012, Ray was chosen a *Top 10 Idaho Author.*

Ray was first ordained into the ministry while living in Orange County and now serves as the Associate Pastor in his home church in Nampa, Idaho. Ray has been happily married to his wife, Sharon, since 1983 and has three grown children: two sons and one daughter. Ray currently lives with his family in Idaho.

www.ingramcontent.com/pod-product-compliance
Lightning Source LLC
Chambersburg PA
CBHW020606130626
46552CB00007B/3063